BLUFF AND BRAN
and the
Scarecrow

by Meg Rutherford
Illustrated by the Author

First published 1984
André Deutsch Limited
105 Great Russell Street London WC1

Printed by Proost, Turnhout Belgium

ISBN 0 233 97629 9

Bluff and Bran were in their favourite place on the sill, watching
Mrs Burke struggling to fit too many clothes into too few suitcases.
The family were going abroad, and Bluff was going to live next
door with Mrs Jolly till they came home for Christmas.

'Now don't you worry,' said Mrs Jolly. 'Off you go and enjoy
yourselves. Bluff and I will keep each other company.'

Bluff liked Mrs Jolly, and she liked her comfortable house, but she
would rather have stayed where she was with Bran for company.

But Bran was going with the family. Soon everyone was squeezing into the car, and Mr Burke was handing in bags and rugs and toys and hats. He was still carrying Bran and some coats when he decided to go back to the house and check that the doors and windows were locked. So he put Bran and the coats on the luggage rack amongst the suitcases . . . just for a moment . . . and went back to the house. Everything was safely shut, so he returned to the car and started the engine.

Then he remembered that he had forgotten to give the keys of the house to Mrs Jolly. So back he went; then he had another quick look at the house, and made sure that the latch of the gate was tight. At last, quite forgetting Bran and the coats, and before Mrs Jolly could stop him, he popped into the car and drove off very fast down the curve of the road and out of sight along the road to Dover.

'O dear,' said Mrs Jolly. 'O well.' Then she turned to Bluff and said, 'Now I expect you're hungry. Come along and we'll find you something nice to eat.' But as she turned she slipped on some soggy leaves and stumbled against a little shrub. The shrub gave way and she fell into the rockery, breaking her leg and hitting her head on a stone. A passing neighbour saw her and called an ambulance. Mrs Jolly was taken off to hospital.

Nobody noticed Bluff, still waiting to be fed. She hadn't even had her lunch. She mewed at her own front door and her own back door, but nobody came. So she mewed at Mrs Jolly's door, but still nobody came.

Poor Bran was no better off than Bluff. Mr Burke had driven too fast around the first corner and WHOOSH . . . Bran had looped the loop and landed in the gutter. None of the family had seen him fall. They were too afraid of Mr Burke's driving to look anywhere but at the road ahead. Every time he turned a corner another coat fell off, and by the time the car had left the town, all the coats and Bran were lying scattered in the gutters.

And in the distance, out of sight, as the autumn fog was closing in and drifting by the houses, the noise of a great big rumbling garbage truck was coming up the road towards them.

Bluff had given up waiting for a door to open, and gone back between the houses to inspect the garbage bins. After a little effort she managed to find a few leftovers in a bag, and gladly ate them. But they weren't the same as her own food, on her own plate, in her own home.

Every day she mewed at her doors and waited. Nobody came. Then she mewed at Mrs Jolly's door and waited, but nobody came. She slept in Mrs Jolly's shed and went each evening to eat from the neighbours' garbage bins, but people often threw things at her and shouted, so she never had quite enough to eat. And she missed Bran, all the time.

She began to wander from home and stayed away for days at a time, eating from different bins, and sleeping under hedges. She found a lookout post beside a field, where she sat for hours watching for small movements in the grass, hoping she might catch something nice to eat.

Beyond the field the wildwood seemed to call her. One day she slipped from her post into the long soft grass, and keeping out of sight beside a narrow track, she went up into the wildwoods.

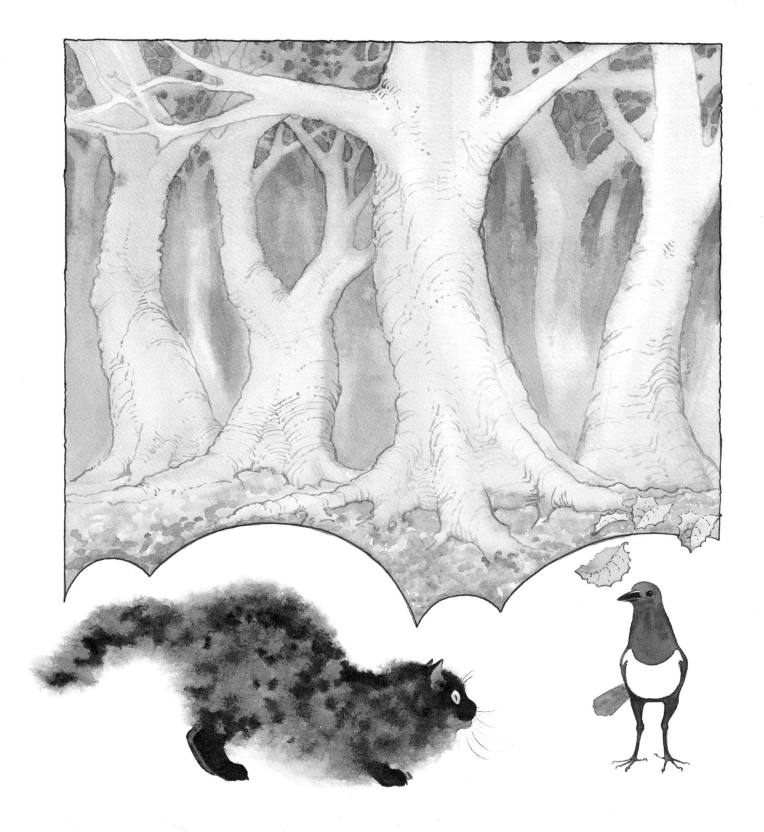

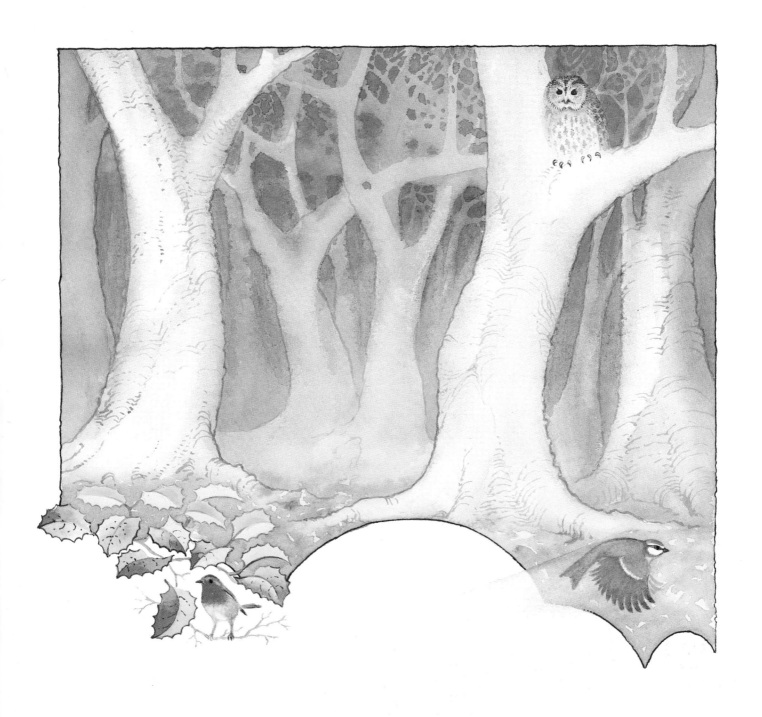

Magpie didn't want her there, so he stood his ground
and cackled.

And all the little creatures ran away, not wanting to be dinners.

Down a lane at the edge
of the wood Bluff found a little row of shops,
with some tasty morsels in the bins behind a fish shop and a
restaurant. So she stayed in the wildwoods, sleeping in a hollow by
some roots and visiting the bins each evening. Winter came. The
wildflowers were dying off, and all the leaves were on the ground.

   One crisp clear day, Mrs Fox came quietly over the leaves and
began to look about for a place to have her family in the spring. She
wanted to be near the bins, too.

She wouldn't share the bins
with Bluff, and she and Mr Fox
made awful noises in the night. Bluff
kept out of their way and, in the early dawn,
anxious and lonely, she went to the edge of the
wildwoods. She saw allotments beyond, with neat
rows of vegetables and a scarecrow on a wooden handle.
She thought the scarecrow looked familiar.

During the morning she moved closer to it, sitting quietly from
time to time, watching carefully. Just to be sure.

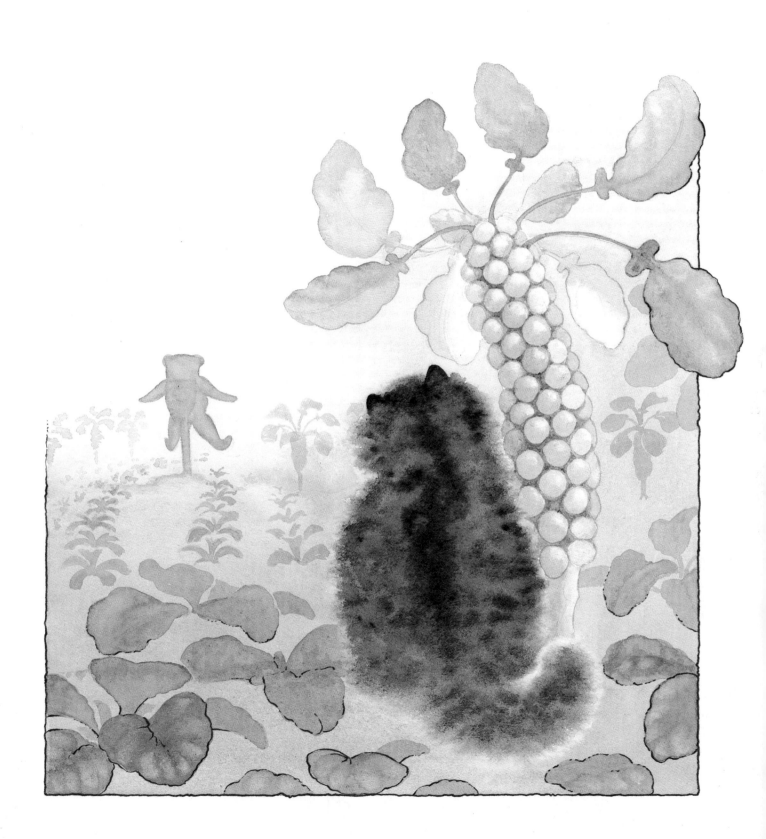

And it WAS Bran!
She was so pleased to see him that she danced
a flower dance to celebrate.

Then she tried to get him down. She pulled and heaved and tugged and struggled, but he was stuck fast, and the more she pulled the more uncomfortable he looked. She tried to dig around the wooden handle, but the soil was frozen, so she gave up and settled down beside him. Soft flakes of snow came gently down to cover them. But Bluff couldn't have been happier now that she had Bran for company again.

Bluff could put up with the cold and the snow and the rain, though a
dry warm bed would have been much nicer. But she was so hungry
that she had to leave Bran and go in search of food. And what trouble
she had! The berries were almost always out of reach, and tasted
horrid when she did manage to eat them. Then her pointed teeth were
the wrong shape for eating the other bits and pieces which she found.
She began to lose her temper.

She was so cross and hungry that when she saw another hard looking thing beside a shed she jumped on it. To her surprise it exploded and she was covered from head to foot in the most delicious dinner. Carefully she licked off every bit, then with a sharp whack of her paw she broke another egg and ate that too. Then she hit the next egg . . .

Now it was Mrs Hen who was angry. She had been away finding
worms near the carrots when she turned and saw Bluff at her eggs.
Running as fast as she could, she burst through some cabbages
and tore after Bluff, clucking and flapping in fury. Her only thought
was to take revenge.

Bluff's only thought was to get as far away as possible from Mrs Hen and her terrible temper. She ran as fast as she could through the cabbages, up past the turnips and swedes and the celery, round by the leeks and the kale, faster and faster, back to the safety of Bran.

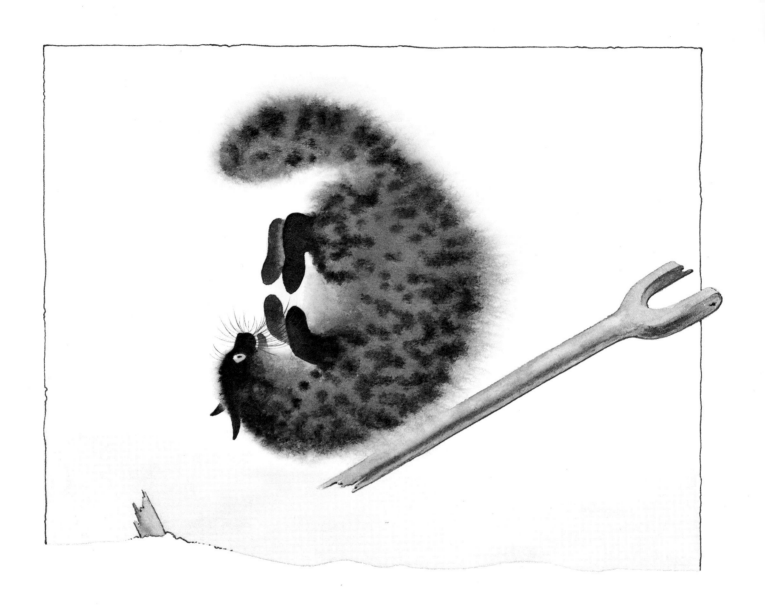

Thud . . . Snap . . . WHOOSH . . . Bluff collided hard with the handle
and Bran was free! They looped the loop in a lazy, dreamy way,
wishing that they had a nice warm home where being cold and
hungry never happened, but where they had someone to love, and
who loved them. And why, they wondered, did they have to be
wandering and lost and friendless just because people went away?

They landed near some cheerful boots, and heard a soft young voice say, 'Mummy and I have been watching you two and Mummy says you are hopeless living up here on your own and why don't you come down and live with us where we can take care of you and brush you up a bit and give you a nice warm bed and lots of good food and would you like that? PLEASE come?'

And so they did.

PRINTED IN BELGIUM BY

INTERNATIONAL BOOK PRODUCTION